To my favorites, Mia and Elijah

All rights reserved. Published in the United States by Random House Children's
Books, a division of Penguin Random House LLC, 1745 Broadway, New York, NY 10019,
and in Canada by Penguin Random House Canada Limited, Toronto. Random House
and the colophon are registered trademarks of Penguin Random House LLC.

randomhousekids.com

ISBN 978-1-5247-1975-3 (trade) — ISBN 978-1-5247-1976-0 (ebook)

Printed in the United States of America

10 9 8 7 6 5 4 3 2 1

Random House Children's Books supports the First Amendment
and celebrates the right to read.

By George Carmona III

Cover and additional illustrations
by Erik Doescher

Random House 🏠 New York

Where does Superman shop for food?

The SUPERmarket.

Why do Superman and Bizarro always fight?

They're not SUPER friends.

Where did Batman get his education?

At night school.

Why does Batman
use a Utility Belt?

To keep his pants up.

What is Wonder Woman's
favorite river?

The **AMAZON.**

Why doesn't Wonder Woman
lock the Invisible Jet?

It's **INVISIBLE,** silly! No one can see it.

6

What does The Flash eat?

FAST food.

Why should The Flash
be president?

**He's always RUNNING
for something.**

Why can't Wonder Woman use
her Lasso of Truth on the Riddler?

He only answers in QUESTIONS.

Why did Cyborg go to the doctor?

He had a **COMPUTER** virus.

How do you know when
Cyborg has been crying?

His **EYE** is red.

What does
Aquaman sleep on?
A WATER bed.

What is
the only game
Aquaman and
Black Manta play
together?
POOL.

What is Green Arrow's favorite fashion accessory?

A BOW tie.

Where does Green Arrow like to vacation?

GREENland.

Why doesn't
The Flash get sick?

Colds can't CATCH him.

What happens
when Gorilla Grodd
gets upset?

He goes BANANAS.

How does
Supergirl get clean?

She takes a
METEOR shower.

What do Catwoman and
Cheetah have in common?

They both hate **FURBALLS.**

Why do the Joker's guests always have a good time?

He lives in a FUN house.

Why did the Joker keep running in circles?

He wanted to CLOWN AROUND.

What are
Two-Face's
favorite flowers?

TULIPS.

Where does Two-Face
like to vacation?

The TWIN cities.

How do Captain Cold and Black Manta relax?

They go ICE-fishing.

Why can't Lex call Black Manta?

He doesn't have a LANDline.

Did you hear about Poison Ivy's new clothing store?

It's called SALAD DRESSING.

Why is Bizarro bad at
knock-knock jokes?

**He always
breaks the door.**

What does Bizarro call a volcano?

A HOT tub.

Why did Batman go to
the baseball stadium?

He wanted to get in
some BAT-ting practice.

How does Batman swim?

He does the BATstroke.

How does Two-Face
tie his shoes?

With a DOUBLE knot.

Where does
Aquaman live?

On a **HOUSEBOAT.**

Why doesn't Aquaman
wear glasses?

He can **SEA** just fine.

Where does Cyborg
go when he gets sick?

To the mechanic.

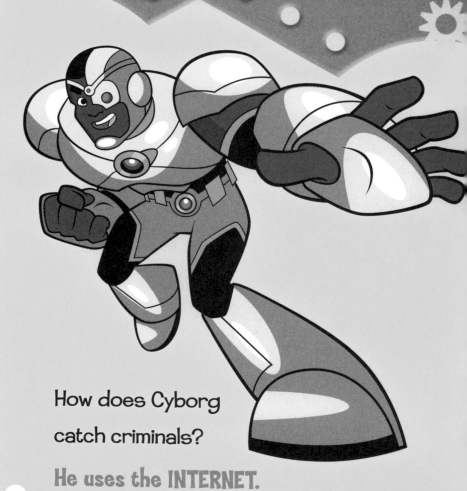

How does Cyborg
catch criminals?

He uses the INTERNET.

Where did Hawkgirl learn to fly?

HIGH school.

Where does Hawkman get clean?

In a BIRDbath.

Why does
Green Arrow put
glue on his arrows?

He wants to make
sure criminals
STICK around.

What is
Aquaman's favorite
kitchen appliance?
The microWAVE.

What is the Joker's favorite holiday?

April Fools' Day.

What does Harley Quinn feed her dog?

FUNNY bones.

Who does Aquaman visit
when he doesn't feel good?

A NURSE shark.

Where does
Aquaman go
to relax?

The WATER park.

Did you hear that Captain Cold
is putting on a figure-skating show?

It's called *VILLAINS on Ice.*

Why was Batman chasing
the number seven?

Because seven
ATE nine.

Why is Batman bad
at knock-knock jokes?

He always sneaks in
through a window.

How does Aquaman
say hello?

He WAVES.

Why does Aquaman's piano
sound so good?

He knows a great piano TUNA.

Why does Cyborg
enjoy the Olympics?

**He likes all
the METALS.**

How does Black Manta
fall asleep?

He counts GOLDFISH.

What is Catwoman's least favorite food?

Hot DOGS.

Why did Catwoman take a bath?

She wanted to make a CLEAN GETAWAY.

Why was The Flash
running around his bed?

He was trying to **CATCH** up on his sleep.

What do you call The Flash
when he runs backward?

FLASHback.

Why won't Harley Quinn eat anything the Joker cooks?

It always tastes FUNNY.

What did the Joker say to the duck?

"You QUACK me up!"

What do you call Hawkman without his wings?

WALKman.

How did Aquaman's parents know he was failing in school?

His grades were below SEA-level.

What do
Superman and
Green Lantern do
before a trip to
another galaxy?

They PLANet.

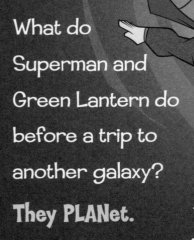

Why did
Sinestro's yellow
ring turn green?

He got SPACEsick.

Where does
The Flash go for fun?

The RACEtrack.

What kind of pictures
does The Flash take?

Anything with a FLASH on.

What does Two-Face
put in his coffee?

HALF-and-HALF.

What do you get when you
mix Two-Face and Cheetah?

A DOUBLE-crossing CHEETAH.

What is the only pet
Aquaman and Catwoman
can agree on?
A CATfish.

How does Aquaman call Batman?
On his SHELL phone.

How does The Flash
like his eggs?
RUNNY.

Where does Two-Face shop?
At a secondhand store,
where everything is HALF off!

What do you get
when you mix Harley
Quinn and Wonder
Woman's magic lasso?
Silly string.

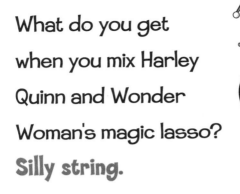

Why did
Catwoman want
to steal
the necklace?

It was **PURRfect.**

What do you call
Captain Cold's
loose change?

COLD, hard cash.

What kind of energy does Poison Ivy use?

FLOWER power.

What list is Lex Luthor always on?

The NAUGHTY list.

Why did Robin wear gym clothes to the subway?

He thought he was going to TRAIN.

What do you get when you mix the Joker and Robin?

A LOONEY BIRD.

What is
Captain Cold's
favorite sport?
ICE hockey.

What kind of car
does Two-Face
drive?
A TWO-door.

Why isn't The Flash
allowed in the library?

**His SPEED-reading
makes a mess.**

Why did Hawkman go
to the museum party?

**So he could see
his MUMMY.**

What did they call
the Joker in school?

The class CLOWN.

Why does Cyborg like to read all his news online?

He likes to stay CURRENT.

What's the perfect gift for Cyborg?

BATTERIES.

How does
Supergirl
get online?

She uses WI-FLY.

What do you get when
you mix Aquaman's and
Hawkman's powers?

FLYING FISH.

How does Black Manta
power his equipment?
ELECTRIC eels.

Why doesn't
Aquaman read
in bed?

**He doesn't want
his books to get WET.**

Why won't crabs
share with Aquaman?
They're SHELLfish.

Why does Aquaman
need a lawn mower?
For the SEAWEED.

How does Hawkgirl
send letters?

AIRmail.

Who is always
asking questions?

WONDER Woman.

What is Captain Cold's
favorite part of a cake?

The ICING.

Why won't Lex Luthor let
Cheetah enter his hideout?

She SHEDS too much.

What do you get when you mix the powers of Black Manta with Captain Cold?

FROZEN FISH.

How does Batman
keep his breath fresh?

BAT mints!

Where does Batman
park his Batmobile?

**Anywhere he wants—
he's Batman!**

What kind of cell-phone
coverage does Hawkgirl have?

Unlimited BIRDcalls.

KNOCK-KNOCK!

WHO'S THERE?

Knock, knock!

Hold on, FLASH— I'm coming!

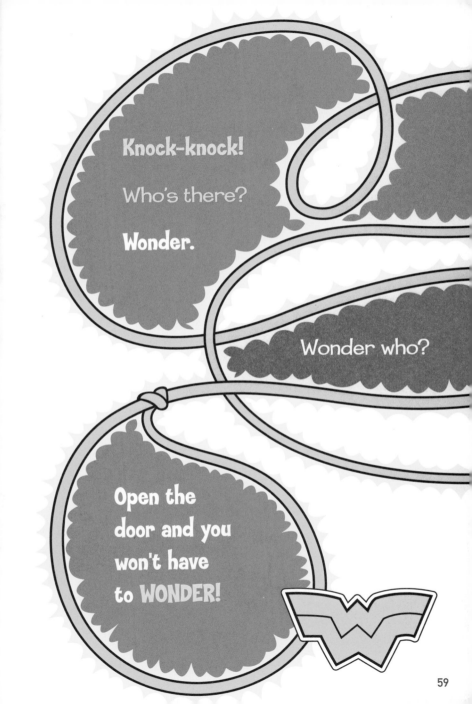

Knock-knock!

Who's there?

Wonder.

Wonder who?

Open the door and you won't have to WONDER!

Knock-knock!

Who's there?

Batman.

Batman who?

Knock-knock!

Who's there?

Orange.

Orange who?

**Orange you glad
I'm not Batman?**

Knock-knock!

Who's there?

Robin.

Robin who?

Hurry up! Catwoman and Poison Ivy are ROBIN the bank!

Knock-knock!

Who's there?

Pasture.

Pasture who?

Isn't it **PAST YOUR** time to go to jail?

Knock-knock!
Who's there?
Stopwatch.

Stopwatch who?

Supergirl, STOPWATCHING me with your X-ray vision and open the door!

Knock-knock!

Who's there?

Bizarro.

Bizarro who?

Bizarro!*

*Bizarro not good at knock-knock jokes!